W9-BSL-162

A Classic Story *for* Every Day

A Classic Story *for* Every Day

HUTCHINSON

Contents

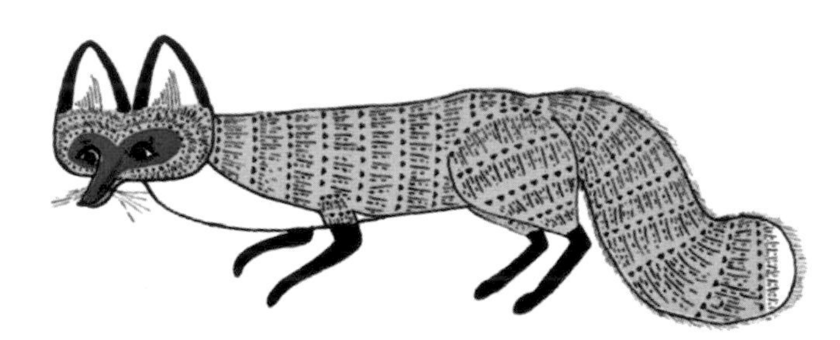

A Classic Story for Every Day

You hold in your hands not just a week of reading, but a lifetime!

These seven stories introduce children to a rich world, both in words and in images. This wonderful world of reading can make us laugh or cry, spark new ideas, enthral and reassure. Children will learn to read with the very best picture-book creators – to understand the language and plot of the story, and to explore the rich detail of the illustrations. They will begin to explore the relationship between words and pictures – where the two support each other and where there are gaps and differences, giving rise to humour and a new understanding of the world of the story.

Enjoy snuggling up and reading together. Have fun reading the story – play with voices and actions, ask and answer questions, and revisit previously read stories with new perspectives. Reading with your child will build their own confidence to pick up and read independently.

This treasury is a true investment in your child's love of books; each story here offers something fresh and new. These tales will become treasured companions to be returned to time and again.

Monday
First published in 1968, *Rosie's Walk* has been charming and amusing children for generations. There's a deceptively simple story in the words – Rosie the hen goes for a walk. But in the pictures we see a fox creeping up behind her, trying to catch her. The underdog unwittingly triumphs in this funny, suspenseful tale.

Tuesday
Shirley Hughes's *Dogger* explores the loss of a beloved toy; it's ultimately a heartwarming and reassuring tale introducing a family of characters, and taking us on a journey through an eventful few days. It celebrates the family and, in particular, big sisters.

Wednesday
Rooty-toot-toot! Quentin Blake's *Mister Magnolia* is an exuberant rhyming story, about all the many things Mister Magnolia has (and, of course, his missing boot!). First published in 1980, it's zany and fun, and introduces a different madcap idea on each page.

Thursday
What happens when four million wasps fly into town? *The Giant Jam Sandwich* is a story of ingenuity and community – everyone works together to come up with a deliciously brilliant solution. With story and illustrations by John Vernon Lord and verses by Janet Burroway, it's immensely satisfying and has a wealth of detail to be explored in the pictures.

Friday
The incredible shrinking Mrs Pepperpot has been entertaining children for many years. Written by Alf Prøysen and illustrated by Hilda Offen, this is a story to spark the imagination of little ones, and empower them too.

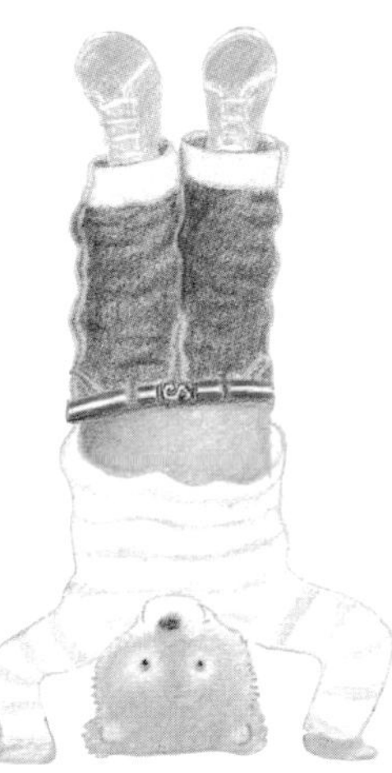

Saturday
Me and You, by the award-winning former Children's Laureate Anthony Browne, is a familiar fairytale with a new point of view. It takes the classic tale of Goldilocks and the Three Bears and explores both sides of the story in a thought-provoking way.

Sunday
And finally *The Bear* by Raymond Briggs. This tale of fantastical friendship explores emotions and humour, and introduces elements of comic strip – a different kind of story and picture reading experience.

Have fun with a classic story for every day!

ROSIE'S WALK

Pat Hutchins

Rosie the hen went for a walk

across the yard

around
the
pond

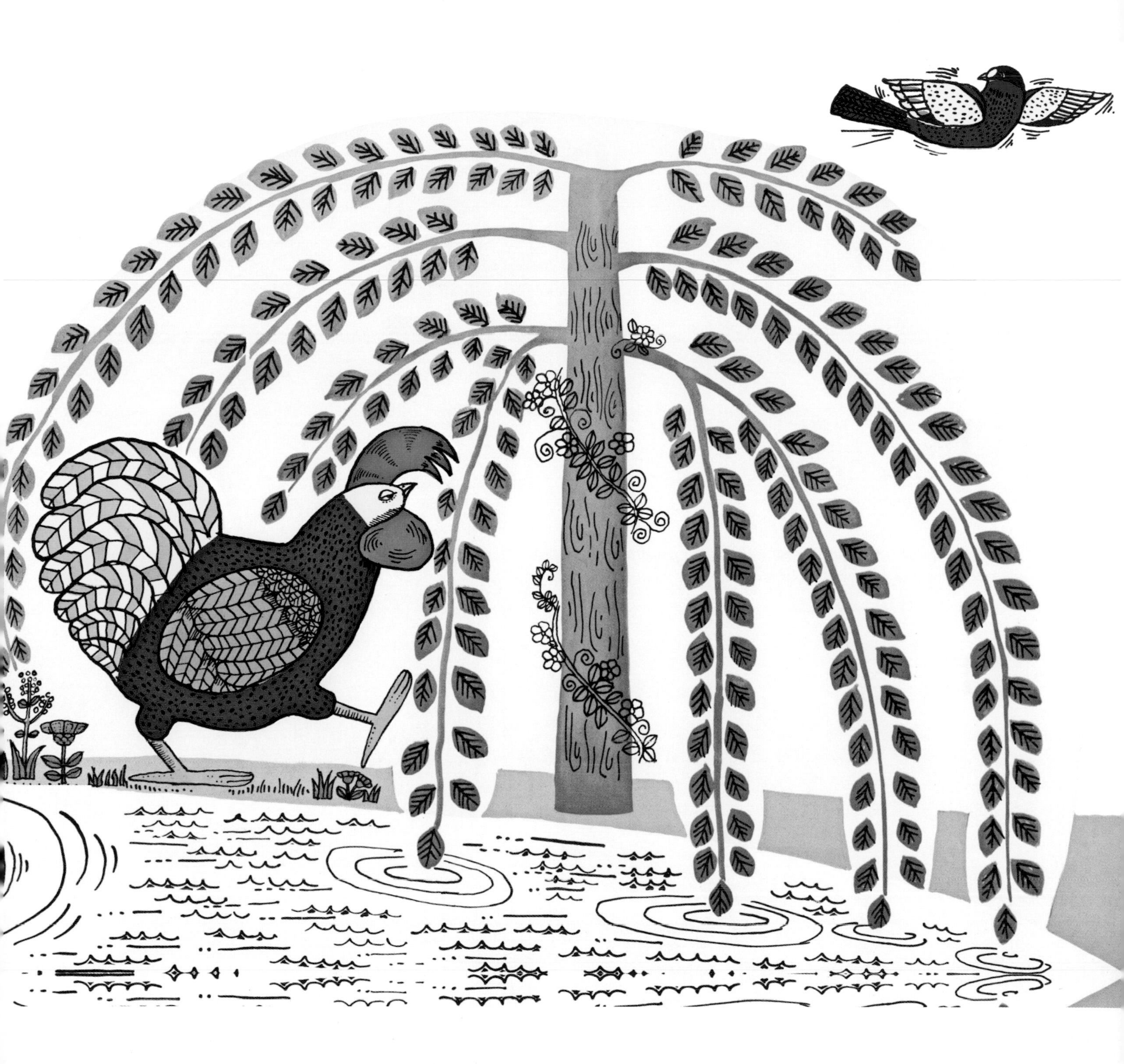

over the haycock

past the mill

FLOUR

FLOUR

CORN
CORN
CORN
CORN

through the fence

under the beehives

and
got back
in time
for dinner.

DOGGER

Shirley Hughes

Once there was a soft brown toy called Dogger. One of his ears pointed upwards and the other flopped over. His fur was worn in places because he was quite old. He belonged to Dave.

Dave was *very* fond of Dogger. He took him everywhere.

Sometimes he gave him rides in a trolley.

Sometimes he pulled him along on a lead made of string like a real dog.

When it was cold he wrapped him up in a bit of blanket.

Now and again Dave's
Mum said that Dogger was
getting much too dirty. She showed Dave how to
wash him in a bowl of soapy water. Then they
hung him up by his tail on the washing-line to dry.

Dave's baby brother, Joe, liked hard toys. He liked putting them in his mouth and biting on them, because he was getting teeth.

Dave's big sister, Bella, took seven teddies to bed
with her every night. She had to sleep right up
against the wall to stop herself from falling out.
But Dave liked only Dogger.

One afternoon Dave and Mum set out to collect Bella from school. Mum took Joe in the pushchair and Dave took Dogger. Next to the school gate where the mums waited was a playing-field. Some men with ladders were putting up coloured flags. Mum said that there was going to be a Summer Fair to get money to buy things for the school. Dave pushed Dogger up against the railings to show him what was going on.

Just then the children started to come out of school. An ice-cream van came round the corner playing a tune. Bella ran up with her satchel flying.

"Mum, can we have an ice-cream?"

Mum gave her the money for two cones. Joe didn't have a whole ice-cream to himself because he was too dribbly.

On the way home Dave walked beside the pushchair giving Joe licks off his ice-cream. Joe kicked his feet about and shouted for more in-between licks.

At tea-time Dave was rather quiet.

In the bath he was even quieter.

At bed-time he said:

"I want Dogger."

But Dogger was nowhere to be found.

Mum looked under the bed.

She looked behind
the cupboard.

She searched in the kitchen–

–and underneath the stairs.
Dave watched anxiously through
the banisters. Joe watched
through the bars of his cot.

Bella joined in to look for Dogger. She turned out her own toy-box in case he was in there, but he wasn't.

When Dad came home he looked for Dogger too. He searched in the shed and down the garden path with a torch.

But Dogger was quite lost.

Dave was very sad when he went to bed. Bella kindly lent him one of her teddies to go to sleep with but it was not the same thing as Dogger. Dave kept waking up in the night and missing him.

GUESS WEIGHT
of the CAKE
???
COCONUT SHY
TRY YOUR LUCK!
5 BALLS FOR 10p
LUCKY DIP
15p a try
TOMBOLA
NEARLY
NEW
HATS
20P

The next day was Saturday and they all went to the School Summer Fair. The playing-field was full of stalls and side-shows.

There was a Fancy Dress Parade.

In this
Style
10/6

Then there were Sports, with an Egg-and-Spoon Race–

a Wheelbarrow Race

and a Fathers' Race.

Bella was very good at races.
She won the Three-Legged Race
with her friend Barbara.

"Wouldn't you like to go in
for a race?" they asked Dave.
But Dave didn't feel like racing.
He was missing Dogger
too much.

Then another very exciting thing happened to Bella. She won first prize in a Raffle! It was a huge yellow Teddy Bear, wearing a beautiful blue silk bow. He was almost as big as Dave.

Dave didn't like that Teddy at all. At that moment he didn't like Bella much either because she kept on winning things. He went off on his own to look at the stalls.

One lady had a Toy Stall, full of knitted ducks and cars and baby dolls in bonnets. And there, at the very back of the stall, behind a lot of other toys, was–

DOGGER!

He was wearing a ticket saying “5p”.

There were a lot of people round the stall. Dave tried to explain to the lady that it was his Dogger, who had got lost and somehow been put on the stall by mistake, but she wasn’t listening. He looked in his pocket. He had 3p but that wasn’t enough. He ran to find Mum and Dad to ask them to buy Dogger back *at once*.

Dave went everywhere in the crowd but he couldn’t see Mum and Dad. He thought he was going to cry. At last he found Bella by the cakes. When she heard about Dogger, she and Dave ran back to the Toy Stall as fast as they could.

But something terrible had happened. Dogger had just been bought by a little girl!

She was already walking off with him. Dave began to cry.

Bella ran after her and tried to explain that Dogger really belonged to Dave, and could they please buy him back?

But the little girl said:

"No."

She said that she had bought Dogger with her own money and she wanted him. She held on to him very tightly.

Dave cried and cried.

And the little girl started to cry too.

But out of the corner of her eye she caught sight of Bella's big yellow Teddy. She stopped crying and put out her hand to stroke his beautiful blue silk bow.

Then Bella did something *very* kind.

"Would you swop this Teddy for my brother's dog, then?" she asked. Right away the little girl stopped crying and began to smile. She held out Dogger to Dave, took the big Teddy instead and went off with him in her arms.

Then Dave smiled too.

He hugged Dogger and he hugged Bella round the waist.

"Thank you, Bella," he said.

That night Dave had Dogger in bed beside him.

Bella was practising somersaults.

"Shall you miss that big Teddy?" Dave asked her.

"No," said Bella, "I didn't like him much really. He was too big and his eyes were too staring. Anyway if I had another Teddy in my bed there wouldn't be room for me."

Mister Magnolia

Quentin Blake

Mr Magnolia has only one boot.

He has an old trumpet
that goes rooty-toot –

And two lovely sisters
who play on the flute –

But Mr Magnolia has only one boot.

In his pond live a frog
and a toad and a newt –

He has green parakeets
who pick holes in his suit –

And some very fat owls
who are learning to hoot –
But Mr Magnolia
has only one boot.

He gives rides to his friends
when he goes for a scoot –

And the splash is immense
when he comes down
the chute –

But Mr Magnolia
has only one boot.

Just look at the way that
he juggles with fruit!

The mice all march past
as he takes the salute!

And his dinosaur!
What a MAGNIFICENT
brute!

But Mr Magnolia –
poor Mr Magnolia!
– Mr Magnolia
has
only one boot . . .

Hey –

Wait a minute . . .

Now then . . .

Keep going . . .

What's this?

Look!

It’s a boot!
It’s a boot!

Whoopee
for Mr Magnolia's
new boot!

Good night.

The Giant Jam Sandwich

Story and pictures by
John Vernon Lord

with verses by Janet Burroway

One hot summer in Itching Down,
Four million wasps flew into town.

They drove the
picnickers away,

They chased the
farmers from their hay,

They stung Lord Swell
on his fat bald pate,

They dived and hummed
and buzzed and ate,

And the noisy, nasty nuisance grew
Till the villagers cried, "What *can* we *do*?"

So they called a meeting in the village hall,
And Mayor Muddlenut asked them all,
"What *can* we *do*?" And they said, "Good question!"
But nobody had a good suggestion.

Then Bap the Baker leaped to his feet
And cried, "What do wasps like best to eat?
Strawberry jam! Now wait a minute!
If we made a giant sandwich we could trap them in it!"

The gentlemen cheered, the ladies squealed,
And Farmer Seed said, "Use my field."

Bap gave instructions for the making of the dough.
"Mix flour from above and yeast from below.
Salt from the seaside, water from the spout.
Now thump it! Bump it! Bang it about!"

While they were working, and working hard,
Some more made a tablecloth out in the yard.

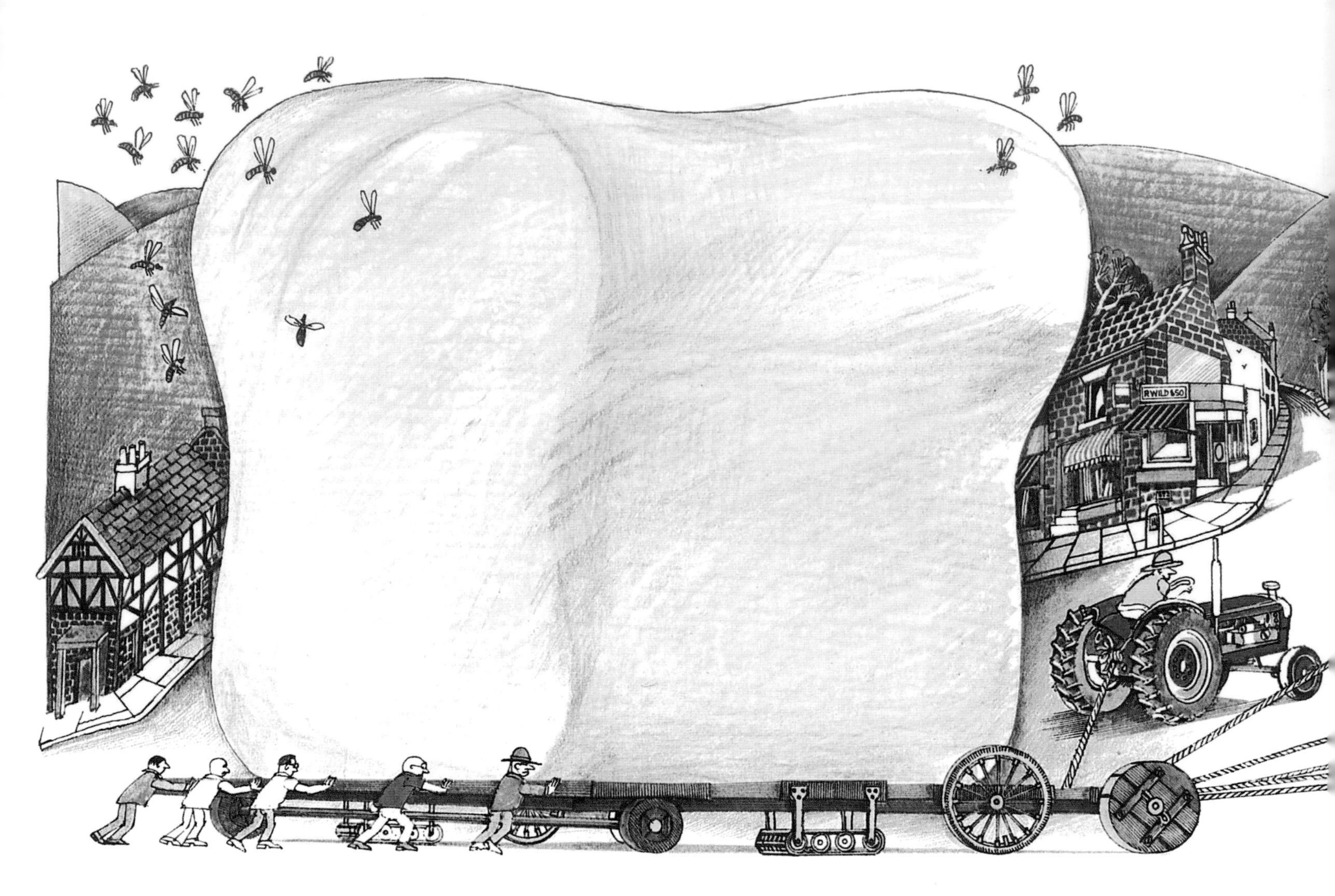

When they were done, the dough was left to rise
Till the loaf was a mountain in shape and size!

They hitched it up, with a bit of fuss,
To tractors, cars and the village bus,
And took it to the oven they had made on the hill –
Fifty cookers in an old brick mill.

For hours and hours they let it cook.
It swelled inside till the windows shook.
It was piping hot when they took it out,
And the villagers raised a mighty shout.

"Isn't it crusty! Aren't we clever!"
But the wasps were just as bad as ever.

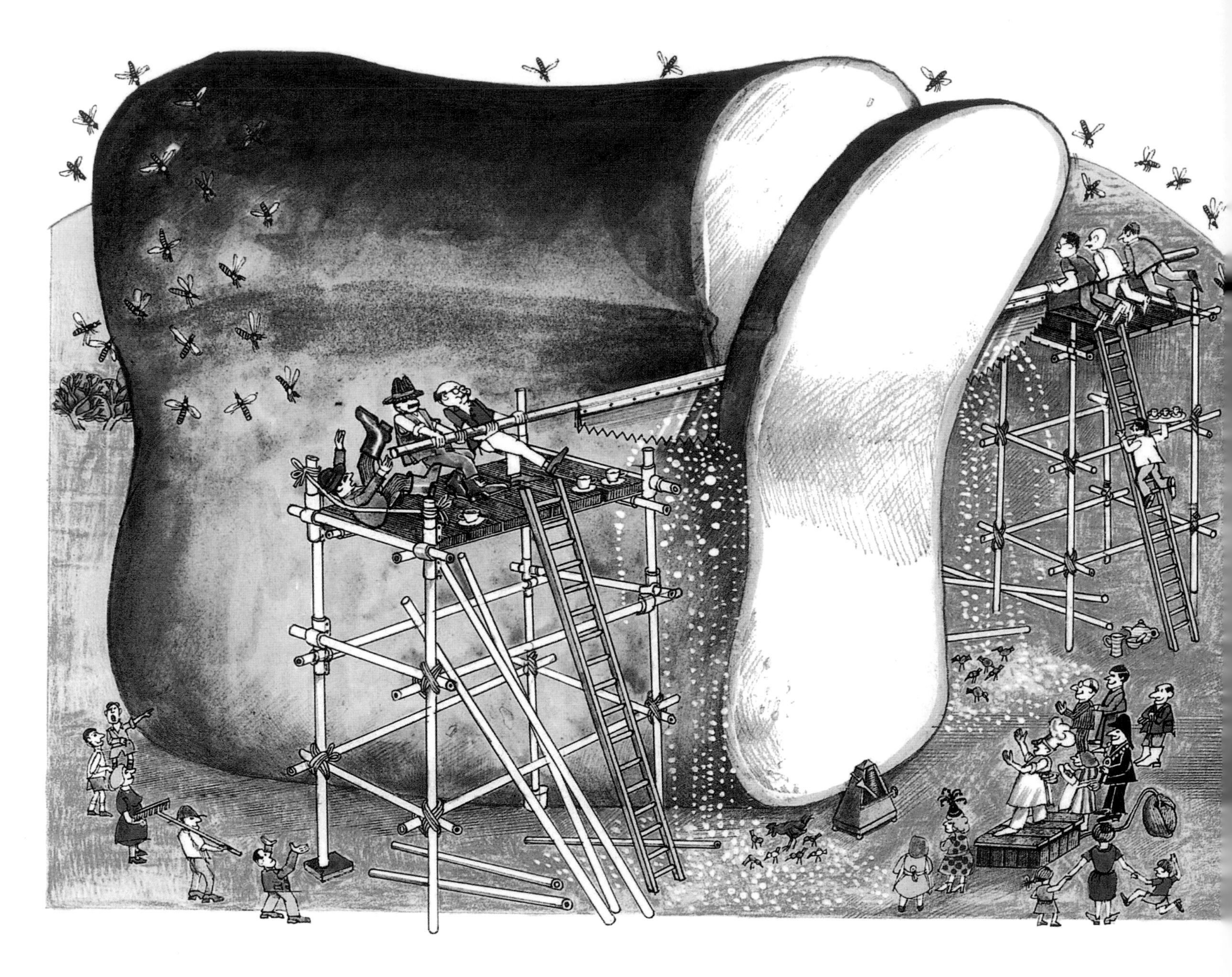

The loaf was left to cool, and then
The people watched while six strong men
Took a great big saw and sliced right through.
Everybody clapped, and they cut slice two.

The village bus, they all agreed,
Would spoil the fields of Farmer Seed,

So eight fine horses pulled the bread
To where the picnic cloth was spread.

A truck drew up and dumped out butter,
And they spread it out with a flap and a flutter.

Spoons and spades! Slap and slam!
And they did the same with the strawberry jam.

Meanwhile, high above the field,
Six flying machines whirred and wheeled,

Ready for the wasps to take the bait.
And then there was nothing to do but wait.

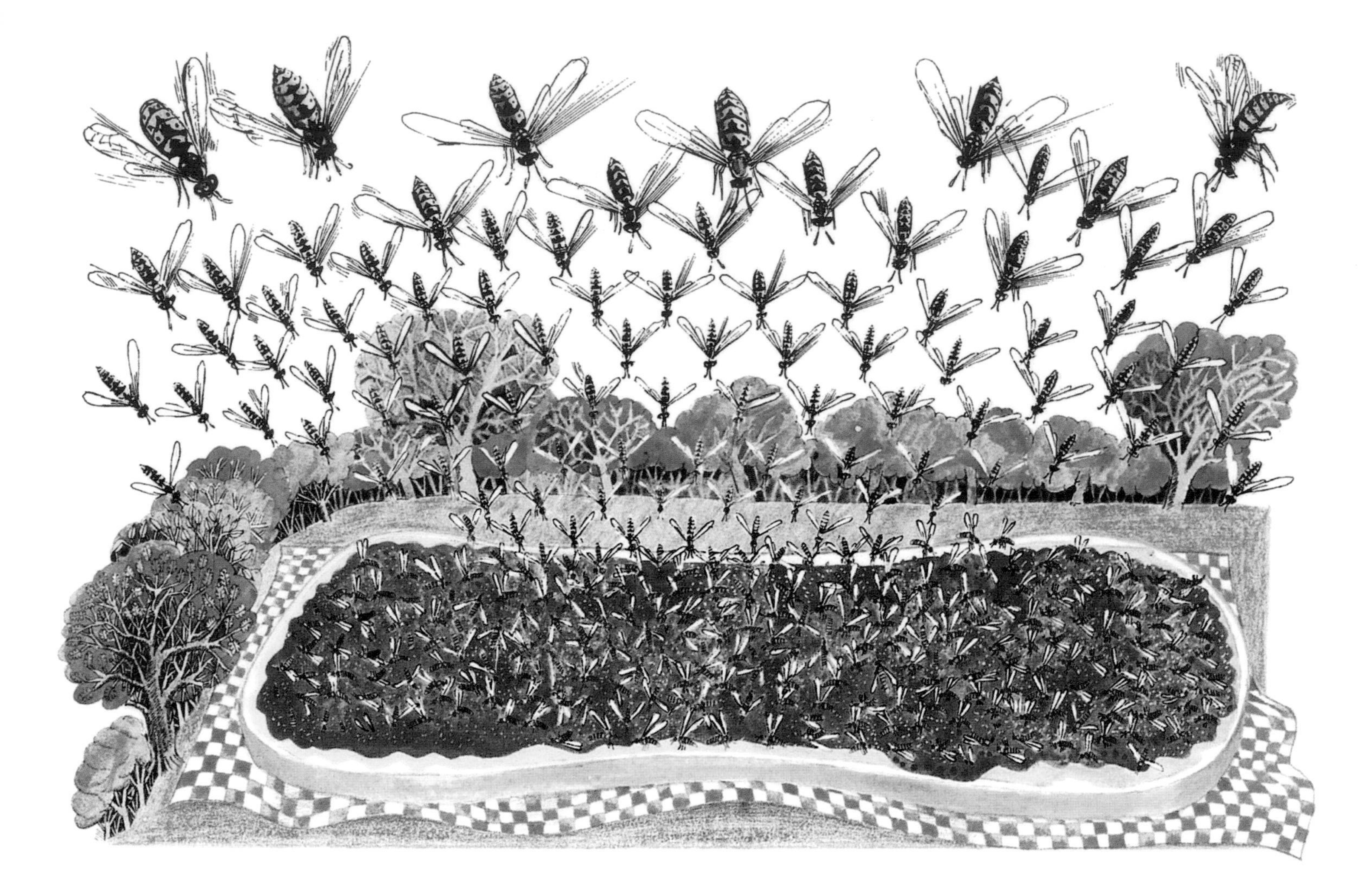

Suddenly the sky was humming!
All four million wasps were coming!
They smelled that jam, they dived and struck!
And they ate so much that they all got stuck.

The other slice came down – kersplat! –
On top of the wasps, and that was that.
There were only three that got away,
And where they are now I cannot say.

But they never came back to Itching Down,
Which is not a waspish sort of town,

But a very nice place to dance and play.
And that's what the villagers did that day.

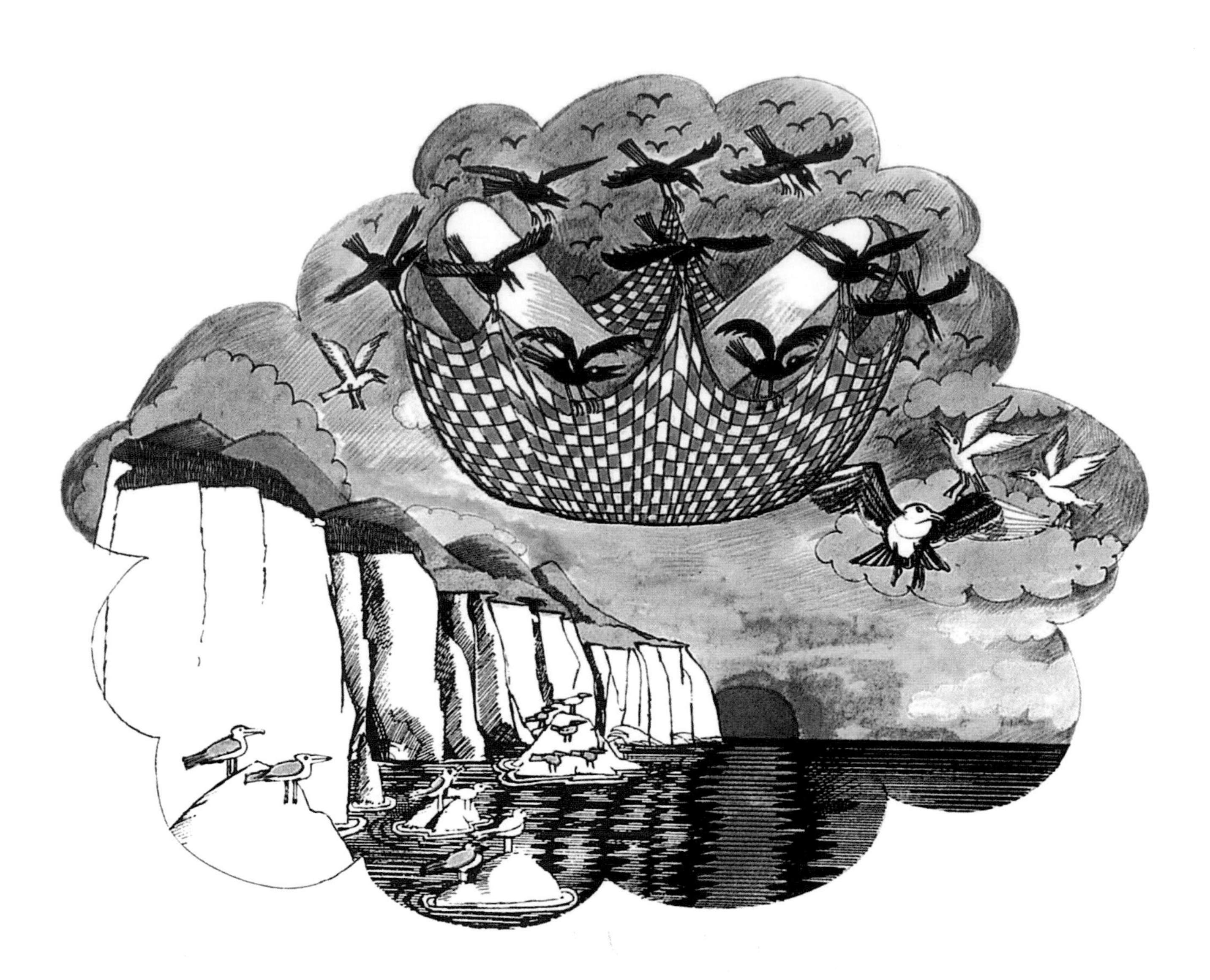

What became of the sandwich? Well,
In Itching Down they like to tell
How the birds flew off with it in their beaks
And had a feast for a hundred weeks.

Mrs Pepperpot and the Treasure

Written by Alf Prøysen
Illustrated by Hilda Offen

It was a fine sunny day in January, and Mrs Pepperpot was peeling potatoes at the kitchen sink.

"Miaow!" said the cat.

"Miaow, yourself!" answered Mrs Pepperpot.

"Miaow!" said the cat again.

Mrs Pepperpot wiped her hands and knelt down beside the cat. "There's something you want to tell me, isn't there, Puss? It's too bad I can only understand you when I've shrunk to the size of a pepperpot." She stroked the cat, but Puss didn't purr, she just went on looking at her.

"Well, I can't spend all day being sorry for you, my girl," said Mrs Pepperpot, going back to the potatoes in the sink. When they were ready she put them on the stove to cook.

Puss was at the door now. "Miaow!" she said, scratching at it.

"You want to get out, do you?" said Mrs Pepperpot, and opened the door.

And just at that moment she shrank to her pepperpot size!

"About time too!" said the cat. "Now let's not waste any more time. Jump on my back and hold on tight!"

Puss bounded off with Mrs Pepperpot clinging on for all she was worth. "The first danger is just round the corner," Puss said. "So sit tight and don't say a word!"

All Mrs Pepperpot could see was a single birch tree with a couple of magpies on it. The birds seemed as big as eagles to her now and the tree was like a mountain.

"There's the cat! There's the cat!" the magpies screamed.

"Let's nip her tail! Let's pull her whiskers!" And they swooped down, skimming so close over Mrs Pepperpot's head she was nearly blown away. But Puss took no notice at all; she just kept on down the hill, and the magpies soon tired of the game.

"That's that!" said the cat. "Now we must watch out for snowballs. We have to cross the boys' playground, so if any of them aim at you, duck behind my ears and hang on!"

Mrs Pepperpot looked at the boys; she knew them all – she had often given them sweets and biscuits. *They* can't be dangerous, she said to herself.

But then she heard one of them say, “Here comes that stupid cat. Let’s see who can hit it first! Come on, boys!” And they all started throwing snowballs as hard as they could.

Puss ran on till they reached a wire fence with a hole just big enough to wriggle through.

"So far, so good," she said, "but now comes the worst bit, because this is dog land, and we don't want to get caught."

Mrs Pepperpot knew the neighbour's dog quite well. She had fed him bones and scraps and he was always very friendly. We'll be all right here, she thought.

But she was wrong. Without any warning, that dog came chasing after them in great leaps and bounds! Mrs Pepperpot shook like a jelly when she saw his wide-open jaws all red, with sharp, white teeth glistening in a terrifying way.

She flattened herself on the cat's back and clung on for dear life, for Puss shot like a flash across the yard and straight into the neighbour's barn.

"Phew!" said the cat. "That was a narrow escape! Thanks very much for coming all this way with me."

"That's all right," said Mrs Pepperpot, "but why are we here?"

"It's a surprise," said Puss. "All we have to do now is find the hidden treasure, but that means crawling through the hay. So hang on!"

And off they went again, slowly this time, for it was hard going through the prickly stalks. They seemed as big as beanpoles to Mrs Pepperpot.

The dust was terrible; it was in her eyes, her mouth, her hair, down her neck – everywhere!

"Can you see anything?" asked the cat.

"Nothing at all," said Mrs Pepperpot, for by now her eyes were completely bunged up with hayseed and dust.

"Try blinking," said the cat, "for this is where my hidden treasure is."

So Mrs Pepperpot blinked and blinked again, until she could open her eyes properly.

When she did, she was astonished; all round her shone the most wonderful jewels! Diamonds, sapphires, emeralds – they glittered in every hue!

"There you are! Didn't I tell you I had hidden treasure for you?" said the cat, but she didn't give Mrs Pepperpot time to have a closer look. "We'll have to hurry back now or your potatoes will be spoiled."

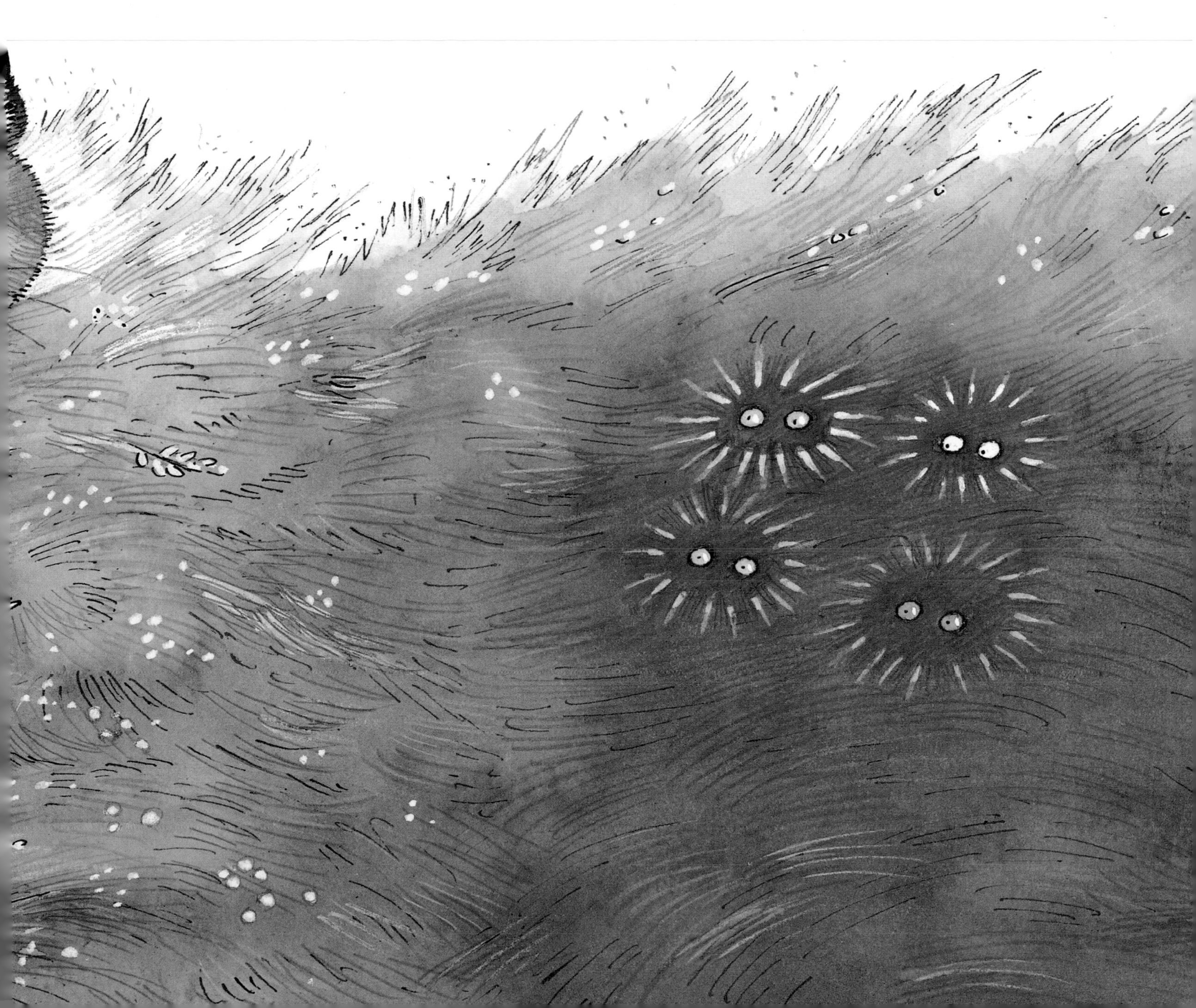

So they crawled back through the hay and, just as they came out into the daylight, Mrs Pepperpot grew to her ordinary size. She picked the cat up in her arms and walked across the yard.

The dog was there, but what a different dog! He nuzzled Mrs Pepperpot's skirt and wagged his tail in the friendliest way.

Through the gate they came to where the boys were playing. Each one of them nodded to her politely and said, "Good morning."

Then they went on up the hill, and there were the magpies in the birch tree. But not a sound came from them.

When they got to the house Mrs Pepperpot put the cat down and hurried indoors to rescue her potatoes. Then she went back down the hill, through the gate to her neighbour's yard and into the barn. She climbed over the hay till she found the spot where the hidden treasure lay.

And what d'you think it was?

Four coal-black kittens with
beautiful shining eyes!

Me and You

Anthony Browne

This is our house.

There's Daddy Bear, Mummy Bear and me.

One morning Mummy made porridge for breakfast, but it was too hot to eat.
"Let's all go out for a gentle stroll in the park while it cools down," said Daddy. So we did.

3

Daddy talked about *his* work and Mummy talked about *her* work. I just messed about.

On the way back, Daddy talked about the car and Mummy talked about the house. I just messed about.

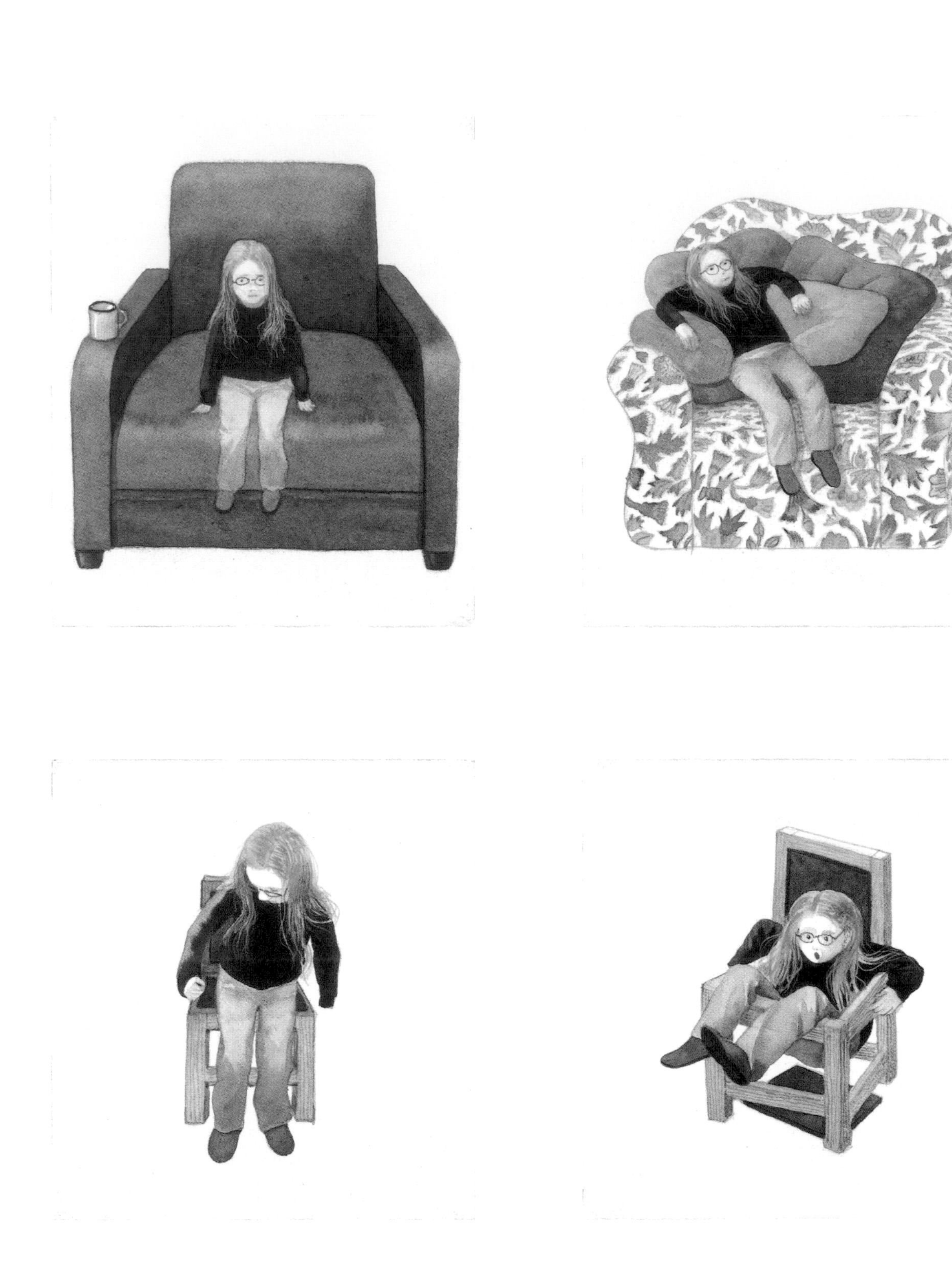

When we got home, the front door was open.
Daddy said that Mummy must have left it open,
and Mummy said it must have been Daddy.
I didn't say anything.

Daddy saw his spoon sticking out of his porridge.
"That's funny . . ." he said.
Mummy saw her spoon. "That's funny . . ." she said.
Then I saw that my bowl was empty. "That's not funny," I said. "Someone's eaten all my porridge."

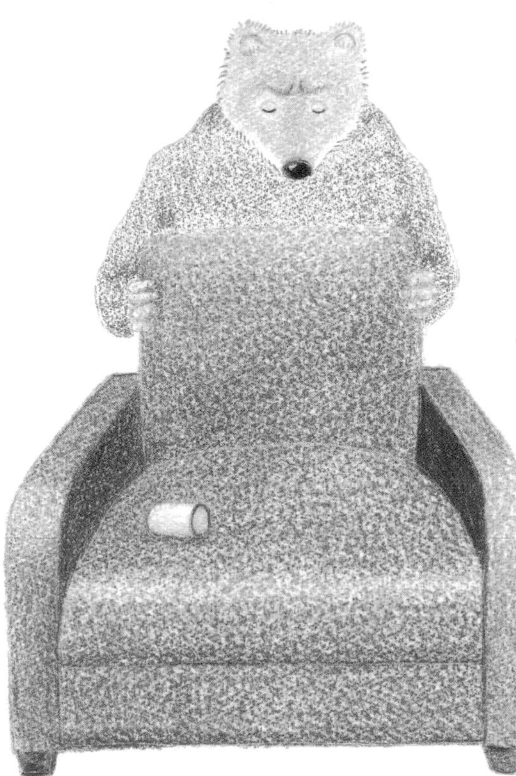

"Hang on a minute," said Daddy. "Someone's been sitting on my chair."

"Someone's been sitting on MY chair!" said Mummy.

"Someone's been sitting on my chair and they've BROKEN it!" I yelled.

"We'd better take a look upstairs," whispered Daddy. "After you, Mummy."

"Do be careful, dear," said Daddy.

"Oh no," Daddy said. "SOMEONE'S been in my bed!"
"Oh!" shrieked Mummy. "Someone's been in MY bed!"
"Someone's been in my bed," I said, "and they're STILL THERE!"

3

The girl leaped out of bed, ran downstairs
and out of the door.

I wonder what happened to her?

THE BEAR

Raymond Briggs

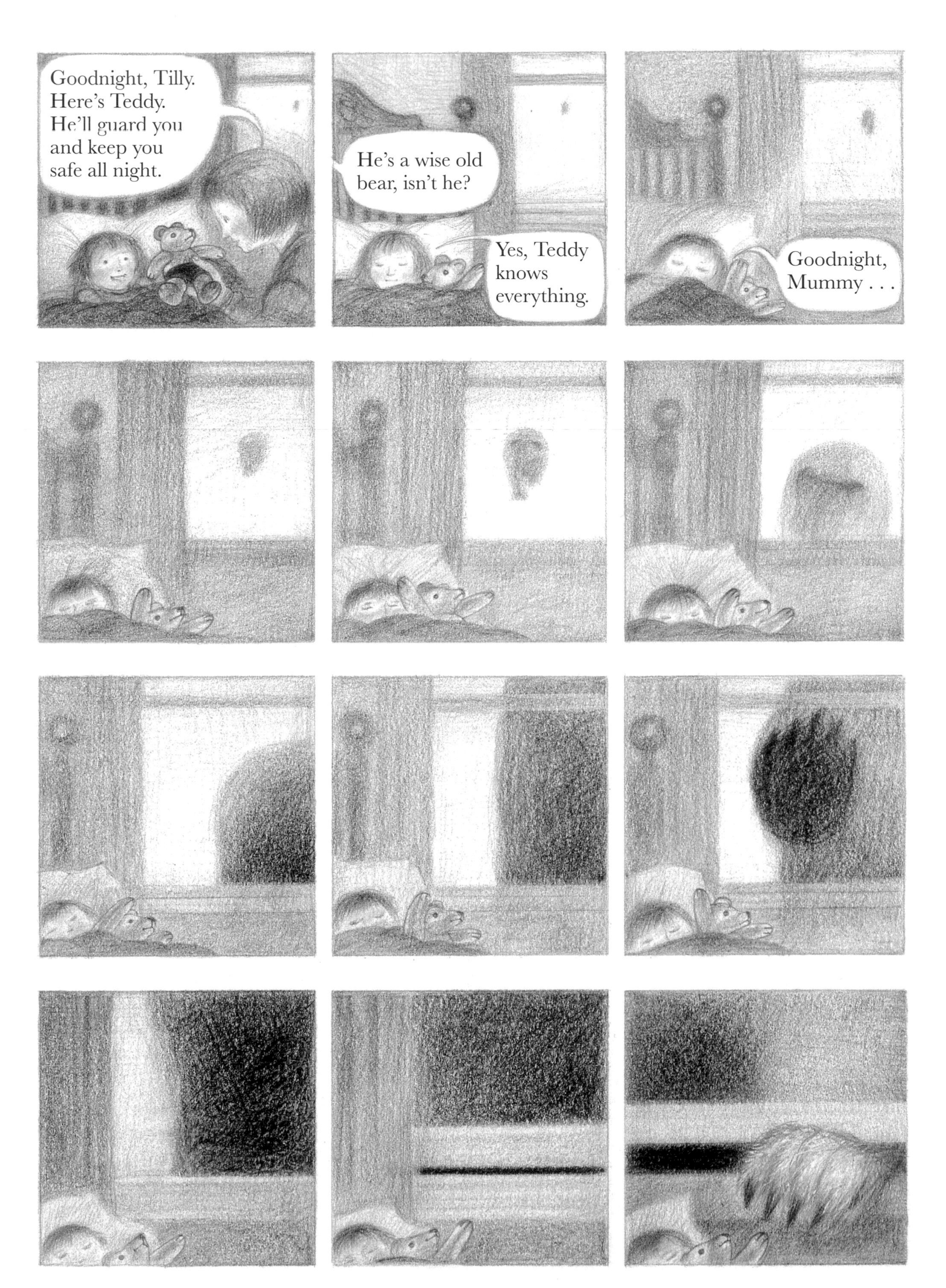
Goodnight, Tilly. Here's Teddy. He'll guard you and keep you safe all night.
He's a wise old bear, isn't he?
Yes, Teddy knows everything.
Goodnight, Mummy . . .

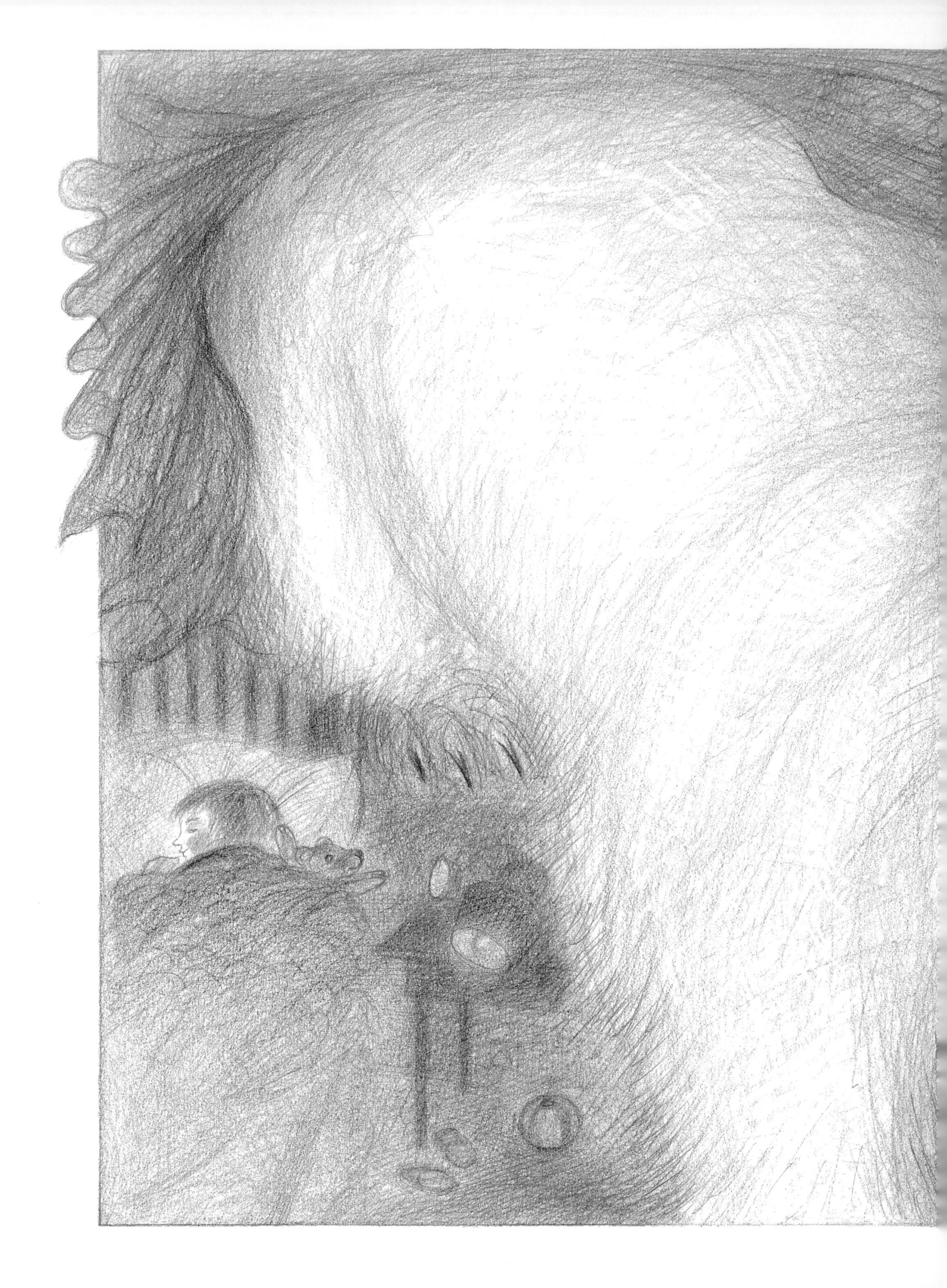

Mmmm . . .
Oh, hello.
It's a bear.
Hello, Bear.

Oh, what a yawn! You're making me yawn, too. Are you sleepy? Come to bed.
Come on, get in.
Oh, silly!

You're *hopeless*!
Do you know that?
Now the other one.
There's a good boy.

Go on!
Go on!
Get in!

There!
At last!
Now move over and
make room for me.

Oooh, Bear!
You're so *warm*!
Won't Mummy be surprised when
she finds us in bed together?

Mummy! Mummy! Daddy!
I was woken up by a bear!

Oh? What a surprise.
Was he a nice bear?

He licked my face with his tongue to wake me up.

Did he?

It was ever so rough.
And he had great big black wet nostrils
blowing hot air in face.

Tilly! That's not very nice.

It's true!
He wanted to be friendly.

Well, mind you're friendly back.

You should see his teeth!
They're all yellow and enormous.
Longer than my fingers.
He's got real fangs.
I saw them when he yawned.
And his claws!
They're all black and curved like hooks.
He could easily tear me to bits
and eat me.

Tilly!
For goodness' sake!

He wouldn't though.
He really likes me. I can tell.

He's asleep now.
I've covered him up
with my duvet.

Did he like the bread
and butter?

He just licked it up with one flick.
You should see his tongue!
It's all black and about a foot long.

Ugh! Tilly!

Can he stay, Mummy?

Stay?
Yes, of course.
He can have
the spare bedroom.

No, I want him to sleep
with me.

Won't he roll over and squash
you in the night?

No, he'll just cuddle me.
I won't need a duvet.
He's the cuddliest thing
in the whole world.

Oh?
What about me?

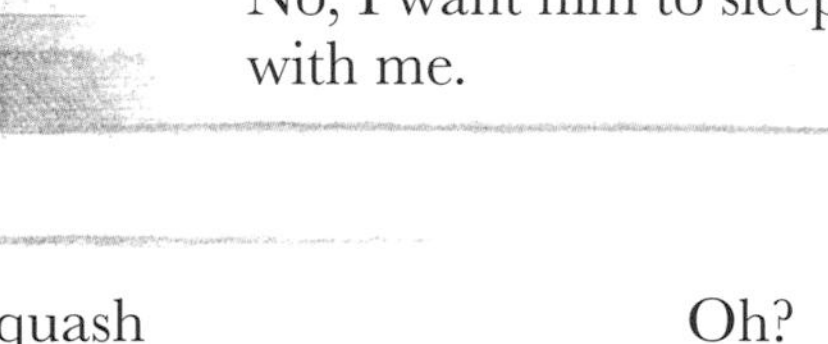

You've got no *fur*, Daddy.
But you're *quite* nice.
I do still like you a *little* bit.

Oh, good.
I know I can't compete
with a bear.

Now you will be all right, won't you, Tilly?

Yes, Mummy.

Daddy is in his workshop,
but try not to bother him too often.

Yes, Mummy.
Don't fuss.
I've got the bear to guard me.

Yes, of course.
I really must dash.

Can I get extra milk from the milkman,
for the bear?

What?
Oh yes, of course.
Get as much as you like.
Byebye, Tilly.
Be good.

Byebye, Mummy.

You will make your bed, won't you?

I can't.
The bear is still in it.

Oh yes, well –
Never mind then –
Bye!

Hello, young lady.

Hello.
Can I have some extra
milk, please?
I've got a bear staying.

A bear, eh?
You'll need a lot
of extra milk
for a bear.
Is it a big bear?

Enormous.

Well . . .
Twenty pints, then?

I think one extra
will be sufficient,
thank you.

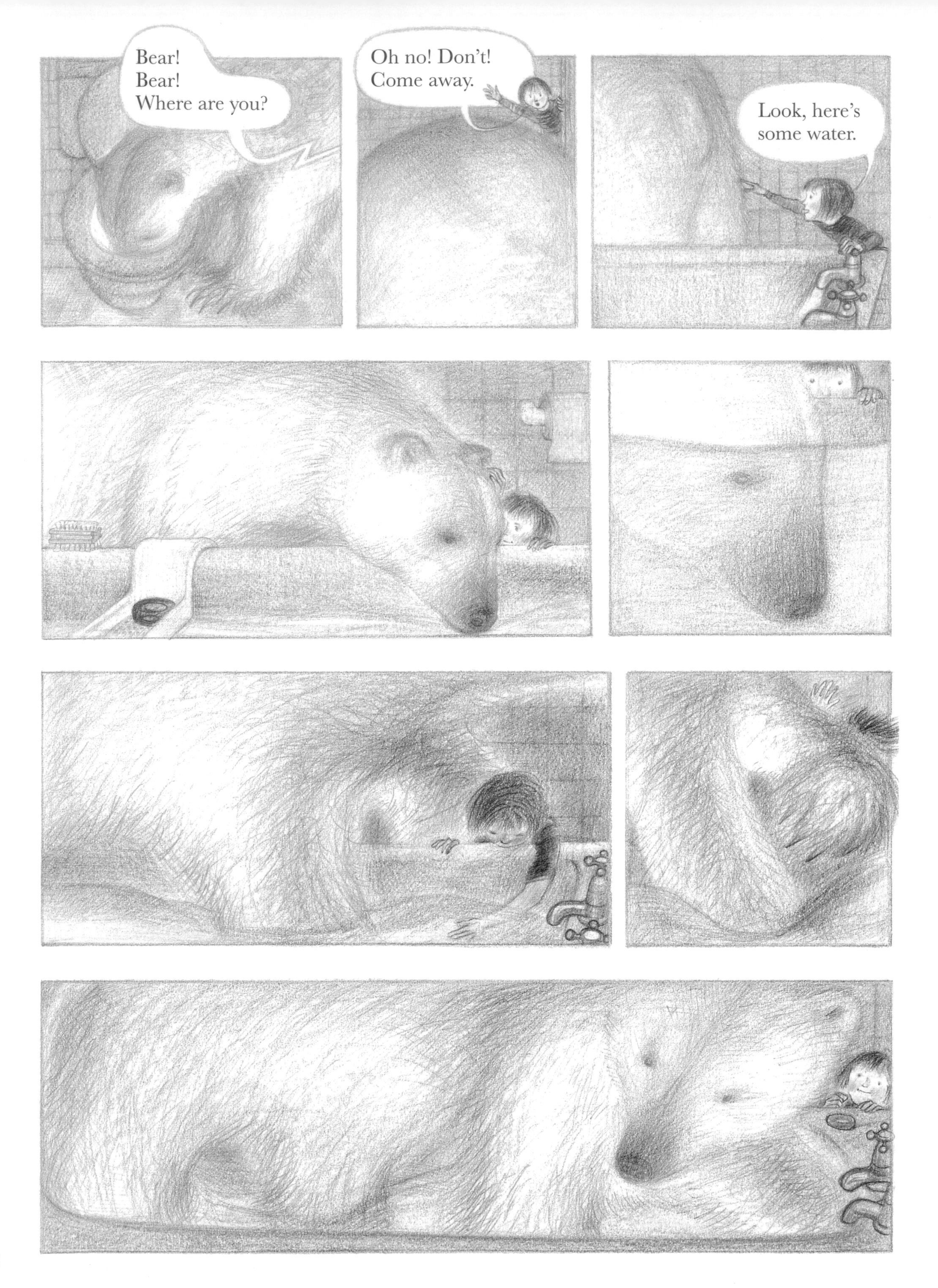
Bear!
Bear!
Where are you?
Oh no! Don't!
Come away.
Look, here's
some water.

Now look what you've done. I'm all wet.

Pear Blossom,
Bear.
You'll smell like
an angel . . .

Keep still!
Don't!

You silly bear.
You've soaked me
again.
I'll dry us
in the
kitchen.
You do cause
a lot of work,
Bear.

I want you to stay with me for ever and ever.

Look. I've got you
some milk.
Now come and sit up
at the table properly.
Sit up straight!
Don't slouch!

Is it true bears like honey?
Try some.
It's Daddy's very own.
My!
You are quick.
It's all gone.
You are a greedy pig, Bear.

Bear! Bear!
Where are you?
How can you disappear
when you're so big?
OH NO!
What are you up to, Tilly?
The bear's
done a poo.
I'm burying it.
Oh, I see.
Good girl.

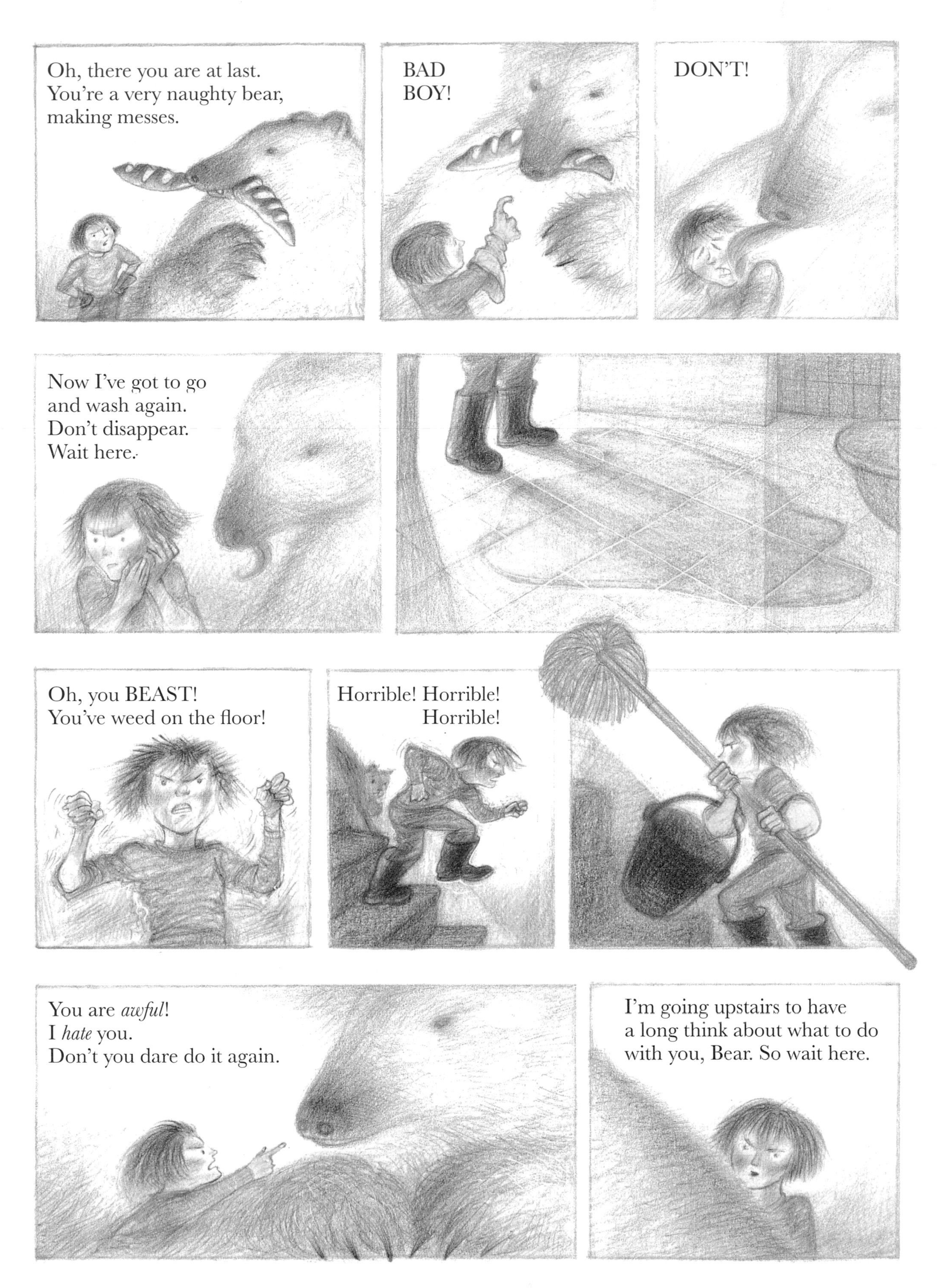
Oh, there you are at last.
You're a very naughty bear,
making messes.
BAD
BOY!
DON'T!
Now I've got to go
and wash again.
Don't disappear.
Wait here.
Oh, you BEAST!
You've weed on the floor!
Horrible! Horrible!
Horrible!
You are *awful*!
I *hate* you.
Don't you dare do it again.
I'm going upstairs to have
a long think about what to do
with you, Bear. So wait here.

Look, Bear, I've decided you and
I have got to have a serious talk.
Come and sit down properly.

Now listen.
You know Mummy said you could have
the spare bedroom?
Well, she's never once seen you
and she may change her mind when
she finds out how big you are.
And if you are going to do poos and wees
all over the house, she'll *never* let you stay.
Mummy and Daddy mustn't see you
or they might put you out.
Do you understand?

Will you pay attention
when I'm talking to you!

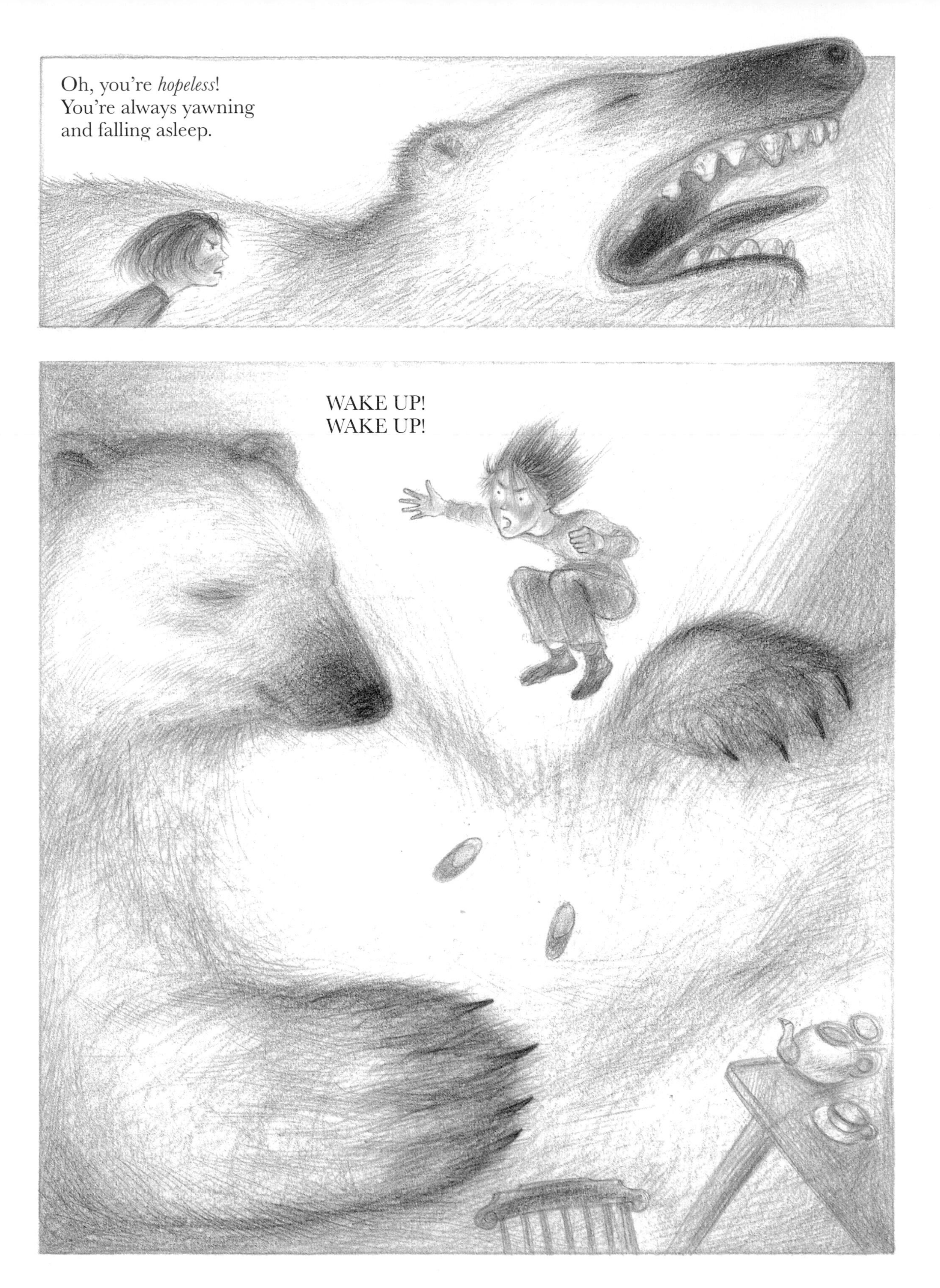
Oh, you're *hopeless*!
You're always yawning
and falling asleep.
WAKE UP!
WAKE UP!

Come with me, Bear.
I'm going to put you in the spare bedroom.
No! *Left* here, stupid.
Up the stairs you go. Giddy up!
Now, you can *hide* in there, but remember you're going to sleep with me.
NO! Not in here! It's Mummy and Daddy's bedroom.
Bear! Bear! You can't hide *there*!
Oh, you silly bear! You'll get such a ticking off!

What?

Sssh! He's asleep.
In our bed.

Who is?

The bear. Sssh!
Mustn't go in
our bedroom.
Sssh!

Oh, I see.
Sssh!
We must whisper.

Yes, Sssh!

He's so big and quiet, Mummy.
He's the silentest thing I've ever known.
He's like a great big white ghost.

Is he? He sounds like
a polar bear.

I can't even hear him breathing
except when he cuddles me.
Then I can hear his heart beating,
too. His heart goes ever so slow –
it goes BOOM . . . ages ages ages
BOOM . . . ages ages ages BOOM,
like that.

Well, I never. He's a long way
from home, isn't he?

No, he's going to live here with me.
His fur is terrifically thick and
when I bury my nose in it,
it's ever so smelly, too.

Oh Tilly, really!

No, it's a lovely smell.
All dark and smoky.

The bear is very good at hiding, Daddy.
Sometimes I look all over the house
and I can't find him.

But you say he is enormous?

He is, but he just seems to vanish like magic.
He could be in this room now
and you'd never know.

Golly!
Just imagine a great
big bear in here now!
I feel quite frightened.

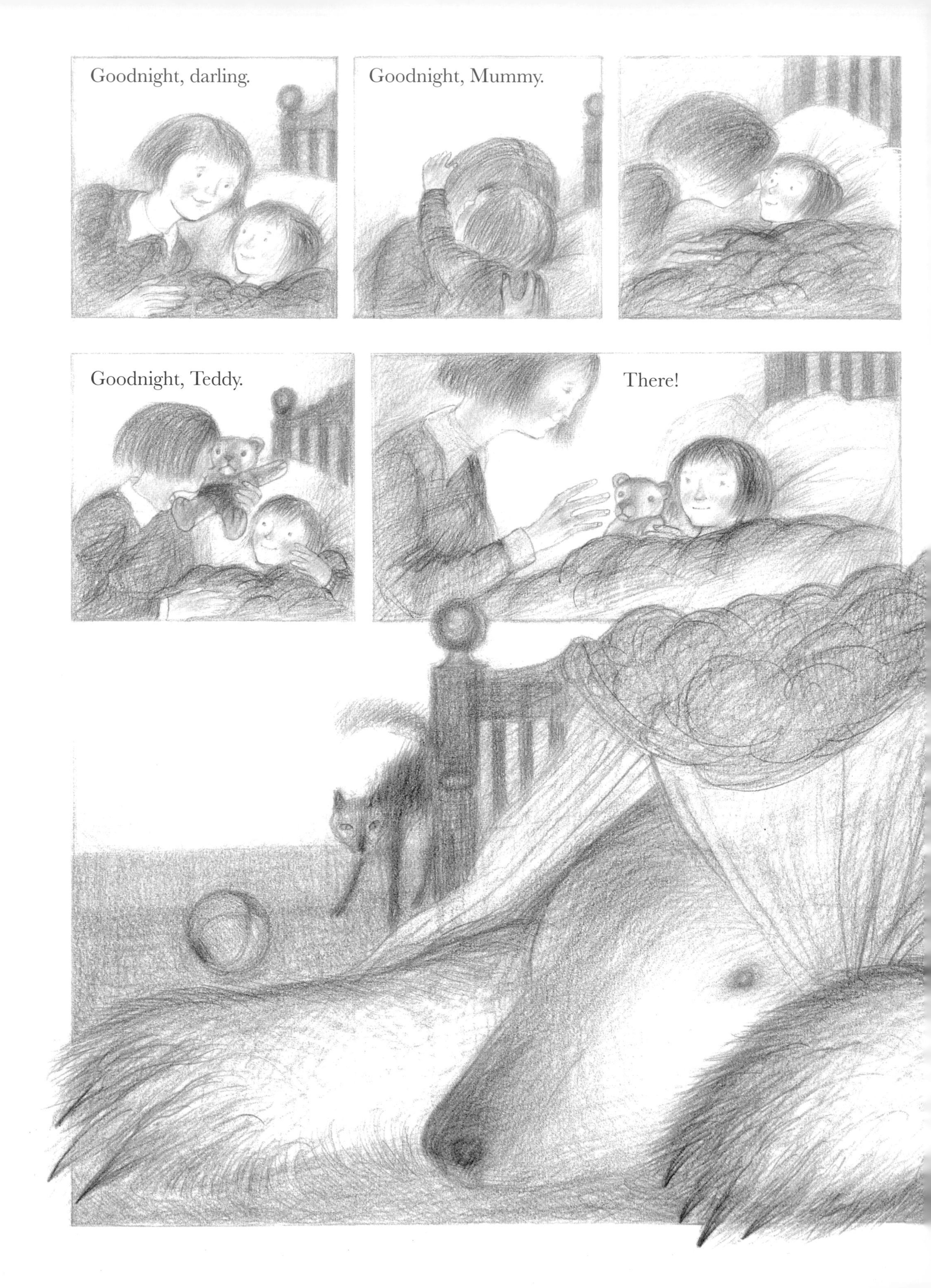
Goodnight, darling.
Goodnight, Mummy.
Goodnight, Teddy.
There!

Now Tilly, whatever have you been up to in our bedroom?

Oh, that wasn't me, Mummy.
That was the bear.

Well, the bear should have tidied up, then.

I did tick him off.
I expect that's why he's hiding under the bed. He's sulking.

Is he there now?

Yes, of course he is.

Shall I give him a goodnight kiss, too?

No, better not.
I think he's asleep.

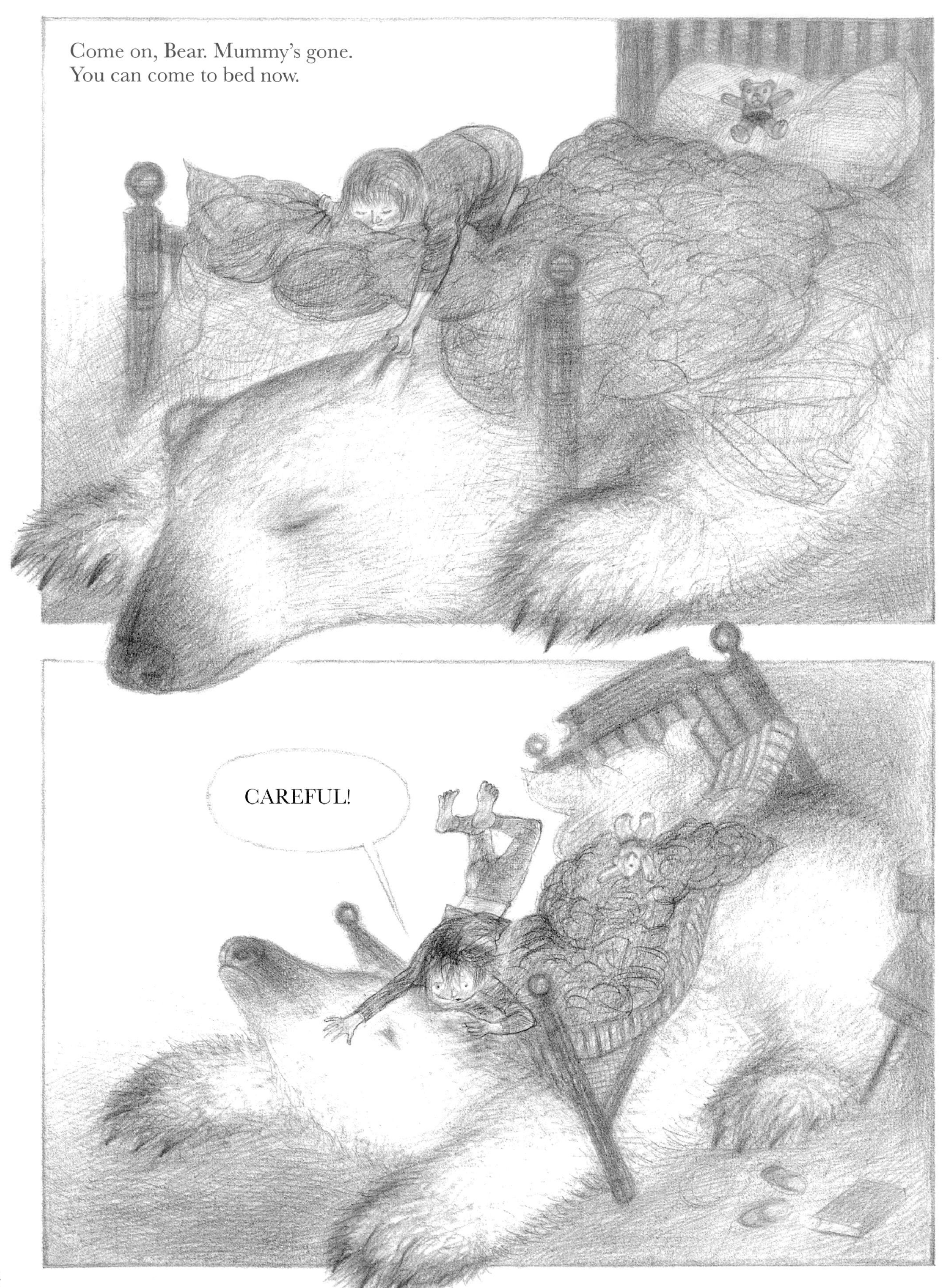
Come on, Bear. Mummy's gone.
You can come to bed now.
CAREFUL!

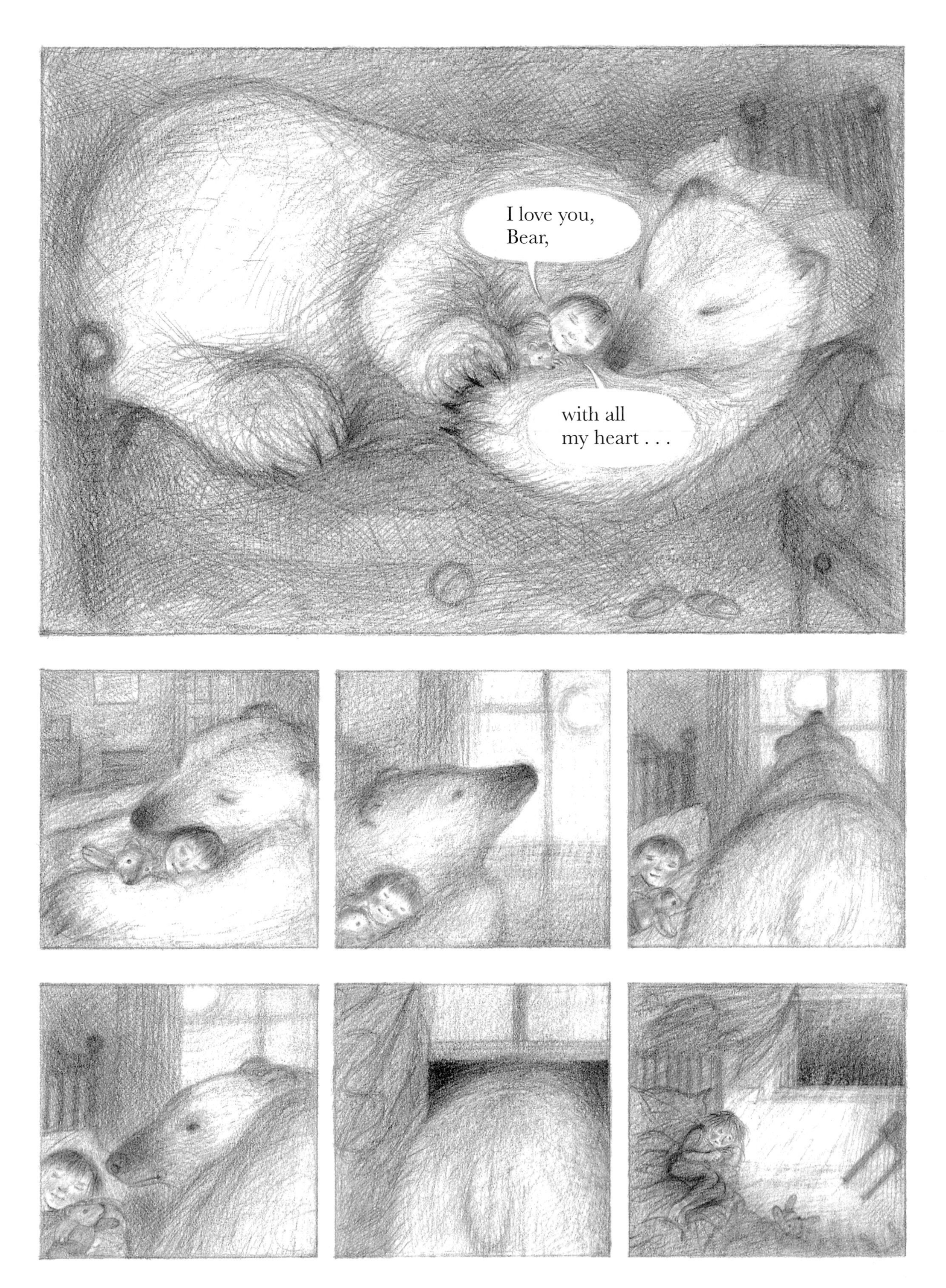
I love you, Bear,
with all my heart . . .

Tilly! Whatever's the matter?
He's gone!
He's gone!
Who?
The bear! He's gone!
Never mind, Tilly, sweetheart.
Don't cry, darling.
Bears can't live in houses
with people, can they, Teddy?
That sort of thing only
happens in story books.
Look Tilly, Teddy's nodding.
And he knows all
about bears,
don't you, Teddy?
Yes.
Teddy knows
everything.

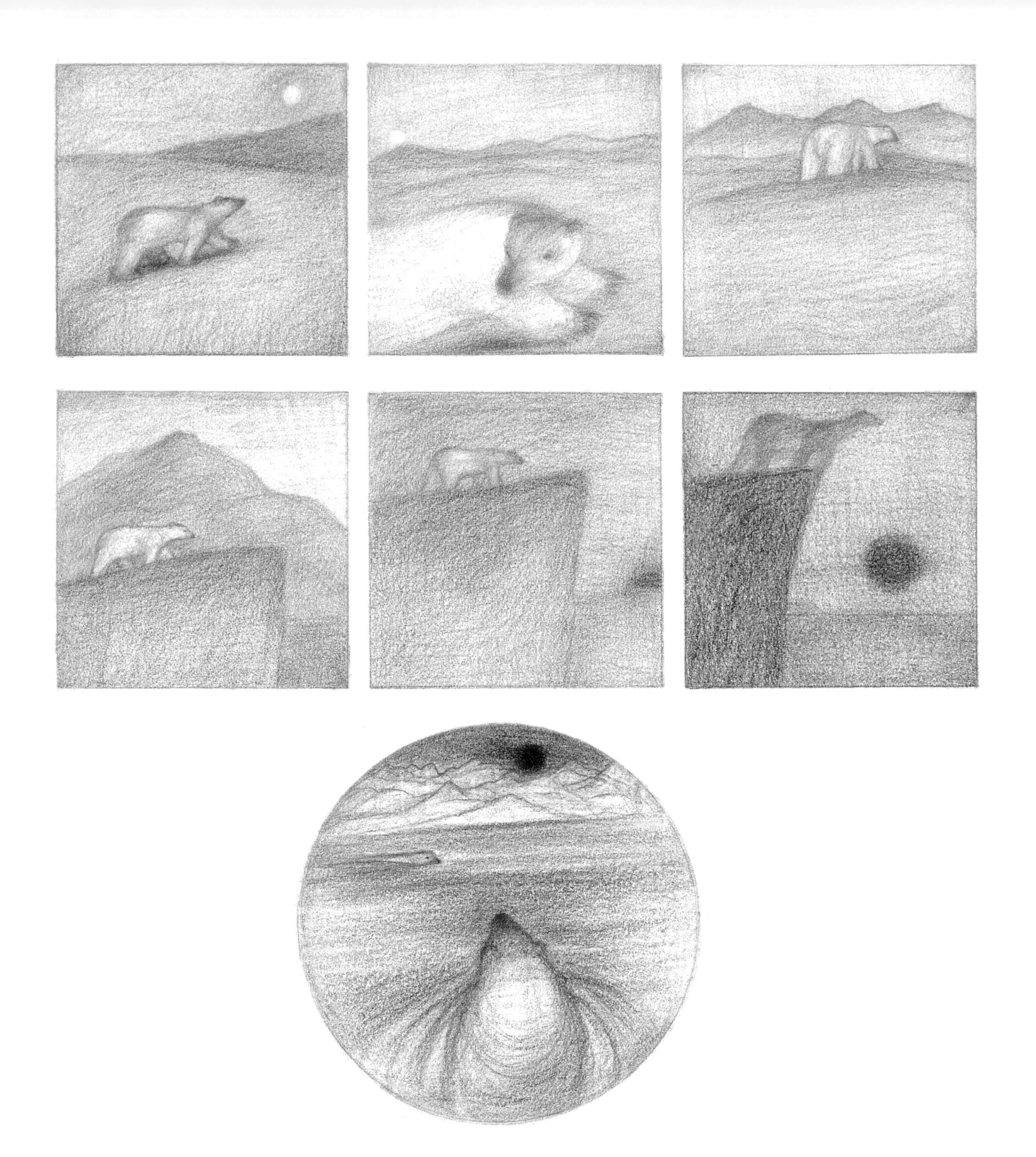

Some other books by the authors and illustrators featured in *A Classic Story for Every Day*

Quentin Blake

All Join In!

Angel Pavement

Angelica Sprocket's Pockets

Angelo

Clown

Cockatoos

Fantastic Daisy Artichoke

The Green Ship

Jack and Nancy

Loveykins

Mrs Armitage and the Big Wave

Mrs Armitage on Wheels

Mrs Armitage Queen of the Road

Quentin Blake's ABC

Quentin Blake's Nursery Rhyme Book

A Sailing Boat in the Sky

Snuff

Zagazoo

The Quentin Blake Treasury

Raymond Briggs

The Man

The Puddleman

Ug

Anthony Browne

King Kong

Me and You

My Brother

My Dad

My Mum

The Shape Game

Voices in the Park

What If . . . ?

Willy and Hugh

Willy the Wizard

Zoo

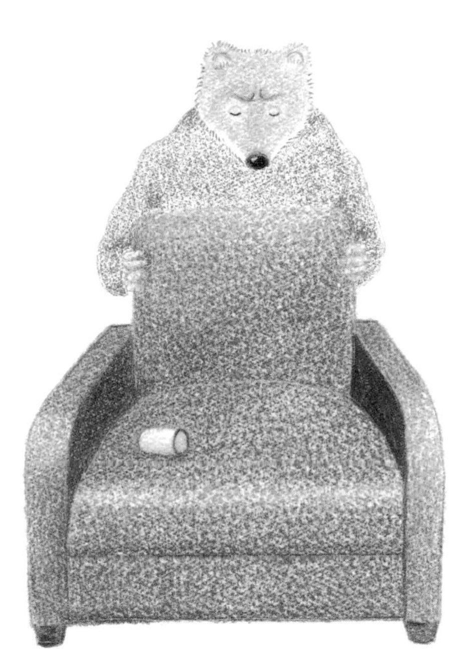

Shirley Hughes

Alfie Gets in First

Alfie's Feet

Alfie Gives a Hand

An Evening at Alfie's

Alfie and the Birthday Surprise

Alfie Wins a Prize

Alfie and the Big Boys

All About Alfie

Alfie's Alphabet

Alfie's Numbers

Alfie Weather

Alfie's World

Annie Rose is my Little Sister

Rhymes for Annie Rose

The Big Alfie and Annie Rose Storybook

The Big Alfie Out of Doors Storybook

The Alfie Treasury

Don't Want to Go!

Bobbo Goes to School

Pat Hutchins

Don't Forget the Bacon

Titch

We're Going on a Picnic

Alf Prøysen and Hilda Offen

Mrs Pepperpot and the Blueberries

Mrs Pepperpot at the Bazaar

Mrs Pepperpot Learns to Swim

Mrs Pepperpot Minds the Baby

Mrs Pepperpot's Christmas

John Vernon Lord

The Nonsense Verse of Edward Lear

A CLASSIC STORY FOR EVERY DAY

A HUTCHINSON BOOK 978 0 857 54016 4

Published in Great Britain by Hutchinson, an imprint of Random House Children's Publishers UK
A Random House Group Company

This edition published 2013

1 3 5 7 9 10 8 6 4 2

RANDOM HOUSE CHILDREN'S PUBLISHERS UK
61–63 Uxbridge Road, London W5 5SA
www.**randomhousechildrens**.co.uk
www.**randomhouse**.co.uk
Addresses for companies within The Random House Group Limited can be found at:
www.randomhouse.co.uk/offices.htm
THE RANDOM HOUSE GROUP Limited Reg. No. 954009

A CIP catalogue record for this book is available from the British Library.

Printed in China